Baby Animals
on the Farm

By James C. Shooter
Illustrated by J. Ellen Dolce

A GOLDEN BOOK • NEW YORK
Western Publishing Company, Inc., Racine, Wisconsin 53404

MCMXCV

There is an uninvited guest in the barnyard this morning.

A tiny baby field mouse has wandered far away from her mother and father's nest in the meadow.

What a strange place this is, so bare and open. How very different from the meadow with its tall, tangled grass. And what strange sights there are to see.

Fuzzy chicks run to their mother when she cluck-cluck-clucks. She gathers them close, and they snuggle in backward underneath her.

A big tom turkey struts toward them, and the mother hen knows it's best to get her babies out of his way.

In the pigpen, the little piglets are sleeping in a row near their mother. One little piglet isn't sleeping, though. He wants to go exploring, but he's too fat to squeeze out under the gate.

A parade waddles by, quack-quack-quacking.
The little ducklings stay in line close behind their
proud mother duck as she leads them out of the
yard and toward the pond.

At the pond, the ducklings swim in a neat line behind their mother, too. Along the water's edge, the geese and their goslings nibble the soft grass.

Meanwhile, the barnyard has become a very
busy place. The little baby field mouse stays very
quiet so no one will notice her. Suddenly the
grassy meadow that begins at the barnyard gate
seems a long way away.

Beyond the gate, in one of the green pastures, cows and their calves stroll slowly among the wildflowers, chewing on grass.

Nearby, a foal, whose long legs look like stilts, practices trotting. He stays close to the mare, though.

High above, a beautiful barn swallow circles, looking for food to take back to her babies. Below, twin baby goats are playing. They bump heads and chase each other in circles while the nanny goat grazes nearby.

There are sheep and little lambs in the field, too. The timid lambs stay near their mothers, and the whole flock sticks close together.

The barn swallow's nest is under the roof of the shed beside the barn. As she feeds her hungry babies she also keeps watch for danger. Her sharp eyes miss very little that goes on in the barnyard. She even saw the uninvited guest arrive.

Now that the barnyard isn't quite as busy and crowded as it was, the barn swallow sees the tiny baby field mouse leaving in a hurry. So does a curious little kitten.

Back to the grassy meadow the little field mouse runs, back to her own house, safe and sound. She's had enough adventure for one day.